A Diamond Refined

Sherrill Evans

ISBN: 978-1-304-15988-5

Contents

Preface

Two teenaged girls discover the temptations and desires of lovemaking and are forced to hide their feelings. This story takes place in West Palm Beach, Florida in the summer of 1984. Ava and Diamond met when they were twelve and fourteen when Ava intervened as a bully trampled Diamond in the hallway of Boynton Middle School.

Throughout the years they lost contact with each other still carrying their secret over thirty years later. Ava relocated to California while Diamond remained in South Florida. One day Ava was surfing the Internet to see if she could find Diamond in hopes of reconnecting. Ava was lucky, she found Diamond on Classmates.com a website known for hooking up folks from their past. From there, the story unfolds…

...1...

Class Reunion

It's Friday and I'm ready for my vacation to begin. "Hun, don't forget to feed the fish while I'm gone." Ava says to her husband Philip. He responds under his breath "Yea I know, now go before you miss your plane." Philip are you trying to get rid of me? You better not have any hoochie mama's in my house."

The phone rings and its Janice, "Yo bitch you outta here in two hours, huh." Don't forget to pack me one of those fine ass Florida men in your suitcase on your way back." Girl, you do not want any of those boys from Florida trust me. The Florida men will tell you a bunch of shit all women want to hear, snatch those panties and never think twice about yo' ass again. "Mmm, sounds like my kind of man, a thug diesel nucca," says Janice.

I forgot you're from New York so you're used to being treated like a used tampon, get used and tossed out with the trash. Girl, I've got to go put my face on so I can look human before approaching my classmates. This is my 25-year high school class reunion and I am nervous. You will be just fine; you did pretty well for yourself. You've got the most traded pharmaceutical company on the market, a good husband and this awesome mini-mansion let's not forget that fly ass Bentley. Call your girl when you land so I know you're safe. Alright Janice, I'm out.

The flight from California to Chicago's O'Hare is one hour and forty minutes with a 25-minute layover, which will give me a chance to call the office to go over the last minute agenda for the next corporate meeting. Xavier, this is Ava

I've set up the next meeting as a phone conference on Tuesday morning at 11:15AM between IVRX's manager Vanessa and Mr. Roberts from our Marketing Department. Sure thing boss have a safe trip said Xavier.

The next plane is leaving O'Hare and is expected to arrive into West Palm Beach at 9:35AM. My first stop is to get me some of that Soul Food that will make you slap the shit out yo' mama. I can already taste the BBQ sauce from The Dirty Spoon, the neighborhood's finest cuisine next to McDonald's.

So glad I arrived on time, now I'm ready to hit the streets to see who I can meet. I called The Dirty Spoon to place my order from the hotel room and the voice on the other end says, "Will this be delivery or pick-up?" I said "Damn we deliver now? Delivery will do just fine; I'll have Spicy BBQ chicken quarters, Macaroni and Cheese, Collard Greens and a slice of Red Velvet cake." The voice on the other end says "Will that complete your order?" Yes, I replied. Ok that will be $8.85 plus a $5.00 delivery charge, see you in 30 minutes.

Let me call Janice and Philip to let them know of my safe arrival. Hi honey, do you miss me yet? Baby, you know I miss you Phil responded. Did you feed the fish before you left for work? Oh! I knew I forgot something; just kidding, yes I fed them. Alright you got jokes let me call Janice and get on my way to Get Acquainted Night.

Let me check my e-mail while I wait for my fiddles to arrive. You've got mail! Hmmm, AOL has some good news for me.

I looked up my childhood friend, Diamond on Classmates.com a few months back when I knew I would be in town for my high school reunion. The email said:

“Dearest Ava, I must say I was surprised to have received an email from you after all these years. I still reside in Palm Beach and would love to get together over a nice dinner so we can play catch up. My phone number is 561-555-0006 give me a call when you get into town. Yours truly, Diamond.”

I’ll call when I finish eating this delicious food. Just as I imagined The Dirty Spoon still got it going on, it’s just finger licking good. Now it’s time to get up some guts to make that phone call to Diamond. 561-555-0006 I can’t do this, let me hang up. A voice had already answered “Hello, hello who is this?” Hi, Diamond this is Ava how are you? I responded in an obviously nervous tone. Well, isn’t this a surprise, how long has it been, 30 years? She asked.

Has it been that long, Diamond? What are you doing at this moment; want to get together for a drink at my hotel? Sure where you are staying, she responded anxiously. I’m at the Boca Raton Rialto Hotel on Blue Heron Boulevard just south of I-95 in room PH1705. I’ll be there in 30 minutes she said.

Let me freshen up a bit. Oh my goodness I’m wearing a hole in the floor with my pacing. I wonder if she will talk about what we did as teenagers. Well maybe she won’t since I am married now. There’s a knock at the door. Who is it? It’s Diamond. Let me take one final look at myself… Okay I’m good, breath check, that's good too. Ugh stop tripping Ava and open the door!

Hey Diamond, wow you're looking spectacular. You don't look so bad yourself big money, she says. How much did you spend on this room it's beautiful, she asks? Avoiding sounding snobby I replied "Not much, let's go to the bar downstairs."

As we head downstairs I see that familiar stare of lust in her eyes. So Diamond what have you been doing over the past 30 years? I'm working as Executive Director of a transportation company based in Atlanta, Georgia. Interrupted by the bartender, "What will you two lovely ladies be having tonight and will this be charged to your room?" Yes, charge it to my room PH1705. I'll have a dry Martini with two olives. Diamond, what will you have? I'll have a Strawberry Daiquiri she said. Do you still shoot pool, Diamond? Just as sure as it doesn't rain is Southern California she replied coyly. Okay, let's get a game going to see if you still got skills. Never one to shy away from a challenge, Diamond quickly said you're on!

She beat my butt again. Diamond you're a pool hustler. By this time 4 hours has gone by not realizing that I had 1 more hour before the Get Acquainted festivities start. Diamond, we have to end our night so I can get ready for the reunion, can we finish this tomorrow? Actually Ava, I'm a little too tipsy to drive home right now do you mind if I stayed until you get back? Sure why not, that way your husband won't have me to blame for any accidents. Oh! I'm not married, she says.

Ok, I'll see you in a couple of hours you'll find everything you need in the top drawer as far as towels, nightgown, and shower gel. Thanks, I'll see you when you get back. As I walk into the auditorium I spot clear across the room Coach Ballard and Michael Vinson the Quarterback on the football team who went pro for the Pittsburgh Steelers until his early retirement due to a knee injury. Out of nowhere I hear someone calling out "Dirty Red" and I knew they were talking to me so I turn around to see my ex-boyfriend Christian Phelps.

We greeted each other with a hug and he says, "You know you were supposed to be my wife." "Um if you recall you had other people in mind and needed space" I responded still with attitude. He glances down at my hand to find a six-carat Princess cut diamond ring donning my wedding finger, then there's silence. I walked away because I didn't want to be under him all night in no form of fashion. Plus I was wondering what Diamond was doing and that's not a good sign already.

Is that Charity all hugged up on Kenny Barrington the crooner from the late 70's? I slowly approached them and before I could fix my mouth "Ava, is that you girl? I heard you're doing big things." Charity began to introduce me to her date, which was her husband. I pulled her to the side and whispered in her ear "Isn't he out of your age group?" She responded" haven't you heard "Age Ain't Nothing But A Number" by Aaliyah she says while laughing.

You're still crazy, so how have you been I asked. Just wonderful, Charity and Kenny responded as he sneaks in a kiss on the neck. Whoa! My cell phone's vibrations just went off, it's the office excuse me one second. Ava Mitchell speaking, Hi Ava this is Markell and I was calling to see if you wanted me to arrange for this package to be picked up by courier? Markell, you're a saint I totally forgot, by all means call the service right away to have it picked up, Thank you.

By this time the DJ is starting to crank up the music playing everything we listened to back in the day from; Sherry by Journey to Pac Jam by Nucleus. Everybody was on the dance floor. Then he slowed it down with a Luther Vandross jam, I heard this smooth baritone voice behind me say," Care to dance beautiful?" I turned slowly to see who was asking. He was fine but I didn't recognize him. I accepted his dance invitation. I must apologize but I don't remember you, give me a hint I asked. He says, "I sat in your Biology class and I helped you dissect a frog because you had this thing about frogs being cute." I am still stumped on who you are. He took me by the hand leading me to the picture board and he pointed out his picture and my jaw dropped.

I was saying to myself," yuck it's booger-eating Cordell "damn he's fine. I played it off, how can I ever forget that and frogs are still my favorite collector's item. We danced, talked and laughed about experiences we both had our first year of marriage. Turned out he married underclassman Betty Pritchard from the same class as Diamond. Oh no! I've got to run; will you be on the cruise Thursday night? I asked. Cordell says, "Yes and can't wait to see you again." I jetted off so fast I forgot my purse and had to go back.

...2...

A Rendezvous to Remember

...The First Night

When I arrived back at the hotel I opened the door slowly to avoid waking Diamond. Pulling back the covers on the spare bed getting ready to turn in for the night, I whispered Diamond? Just to see if she was really asleep. I got no answer so I turned over and off to sleep I went. I later felt a draft and cold feet against my calf; I began to sweat because I now had company in my bed that wasn't Philip.

Diamond whispers "Did you ever think about me over the years?" I couldn't lie because I did think about her, so I said "Yes I did." Then it became a series of questions; what did you think about, did you ever tell anyone our secret, do you ever think about what it would be like being with each other again today? Blushing, I nodded my head because by then I was feeling like some five-year old who just got kissed for the first time.

I thought you were sleep, Diamond. I was until you came in, do you mind me lying next to you, she says. As much as I wanted to say I do mind now move back to the other bed, the words couldn't come out my mouth. I don't mind Diamond… We lay together and talked until 3AM about the days of old. Do you remember when we first kissed? I asked. Girl, how could I ever forget that? Ava, you were so nervous you bit your own tongue, Diamond boasted.

I must confess something to you, Diamond. I have been with two other women after you so I had become quite the romancer then but that was a long time ago, I changed and I just don't have that same passion for my husband. Your what? Diamond said shocked. Oh I didn't tell you? I'm married now. I've been married for six years; his name is Philip Mitchell. Do you have any children yet? She asked. I have no children.

Diamond says "did you tell those other two women about us?" Hell to da naw! I asserted, I told nobody of our secret. Diamond, I still love you or should I say I'm still in love with you and I'm afraid if I allow my feelings to run me I won't be able to contain myself. Ava, let it go, how often do we see each other? Oh Diamond, you really don't know what you're asking of me, you will get hooked and we'll be back at a new beginning. I've never known you to be a quitter Ava don't make me go another 30 years without knowing what it would be like to be with you again.

I jumped up from the bed, wrestling with the proposition before me. As I walked to the bathroom I said to myself, "what the fuck you only live once." Diamond followed and wrapped her arms around my waist and says "I've waited for this moment for 30 years." Holding onto one of her arms I spun around to face her and planted a wet kiss on her ever so supple lips with a slight swivel of the hips. She began to moan and I knew she was mine all over again. We made a dash for the bed undressing each other and I began to nibble on her inner-thighs. Diamond says to me "What are you doing down there?" I laughed and asked her if she's still a virgin to all sexual aspects? To which she replied, something like that. That shit turned me on even more, I can't lie… I'll tell you what just lay back relax and allow me to bring you up to speed.

I resumed nibbling on her inner-thighs and caressing her nipples. I reached down to her dark, warm, moist pit and began stroking it gently. I noticed the clitoris swelling which was my signal to stroke it with my tongue. I alternated my licking, sucking with a pulling action; the moans got louder I wasn't ready for her to climax yet so I stopped and sucked on her nipples while hand massaging her pussy.

Diamond started to wiggle with anticipation; therefore it was time to make her cum. I returned to licking and sucking her clit, the wetness was unbelievable. She climaxed almost instantly while I continued to catch all of the essence of her in my mouth. I then straddled myself on top of her to join in on the passionate feeling; positioning my wet pussy inside of hers as close as possible and began to grind. I felt my clit throbbing along with Diamond's. We both began to hold each other tighter until we climaxed together and tears of pure passion and love fell from my eyes.

Our eyes locked and we both knew we had just opened Pandora's Box all over again. Ava, I've never felt so good and I can't believe you're clear across the country with a husband after that love making session. Diamond, I told you this would be the outcome if we made love. Now how am I gonna go home and try not think about making love to you while having sex with Philip?

Fuck Philip I had you first, she says. Diamond, you will always have me for life. Leave your husband and come back to Florida so we can be together. After making love with you I'm liable to lose my mind and do just that, leave Philip and move the company to Fort Lauderdale. Diamond wobbled over to the bathroom sink saying" Damn, Damn, Damn." I chuckled, "what's wrong Florida Evans?" My ego was saying, "Girl you still got the stroke and the rhythm" while sporting a cheese eating grin on my face. I was feeling aiight than a motherfucker.

Ava? "Yes, Diamond?" You mean to tell me you've learned all of this with two women and you decided to give it all up and marry a man, why?" Well, to be honest I thought it was the right thing to do for my image. Society has this PC image of; Corporate American heterosexuals and how we're to live. They didn't factor in the other lifestyles such as gays and lesbians. I just got caught up in their beliefs when I became the business person I am, as a successful African American female and that's just unheard of in Corporate America.

Ava, it's not fair that people have so much influence on how you're supposed to live your life without being judged. They just don't know there's a bigger judge and a bigger judgment day approaching and neither of these people here will be behind the pulpit when I get my turn. I just wish people would just mind their business instead of others, and then maybe they won't be so miserable themselves, Diamond replied as she returned to bed. When I am with Philip sexually I understand what Celie from the Color Purple was feeling, just climb up and do his business and a few seconds later he's off to sleep.

Bursting out in laughter, Diamond says "Baby, I won't do that to you if you just teach me." I just might take you up on that baby-girl, I will teach you anything you want as long as you show me the same amount of affection and reciprocate what I give to you. A relationship consist of two parties therefore it's not 60-40 it needs to be 50/50 in order for it to grow and prosper. I think I can handle that Ava just give us a chance.

My lips began to glide across the nape of Diamond's neck while spooning, "good morning sunshine, its 5 O'clock let's get some shut eye and we'll go to breakfast when we wake," I said. It was complete silence thereafter she had fallen off to sleep in my arms. I lay awake for the next thirty minutes with things flying through my mind. I love Diamond very much I now realize she was the missing piece to my happiness and now that we've found each other it's no telling how things will change when I get home. I can surely go to sleep and wake up with Diamond for the rest of my life.

...The Morning After

Rise and shine my Sleeping Beauty this soft voice whispered in my ears. Not opening an eye I flash a broad smile responding "good morning Diamond." Let's shower together before breakfast she said. I opened my eyes and to my surprise Diamond was already naked. Mmmm, you're a damn good sight for sore eyes. She took me by the hand and led me to the shower. As she stood beneath the spout, I stood back and carefully studied her body, the water saturated every curve and soon our hot shower became filled with moans of pleasure until at last, Diamond once again exploded at my touch. Now, I'm really hungry, she said grinning with satisfaction. What do you want to eat?" I replied how about a nice island breakfast I know of a Jamaican restaurant in Ft. Lauderdale on Oakland Park Blvd. Mmm! A Jamaican breakfast sounds good; smothered liver with onions or even Salt fish and akee. We got dressed and out we went, let's ride little lady my car is in the garage I'll drive, she said.

We arrive at a place called Café Calypso and it has such great ambiance. Reggae music playing in the background, very dim lighting and very cordial waiters and waitresses just made it easy to relax and enjoy. I've heard stories of how in Jamaica being gay is not tolerated so I had to curb my lustful eyes from gazing into Diamond's beautiful chestnut brown almond shaped eyes. The waiter comes to the table greets us like "Good morning ladies my name is June-ya (Junior) I'll be your waita tu-day can I start you wit a nice cold glass of Ting, Ginga Beer or Punch?" Diamond says" I'll have the

Ginger Beer but feeling like Red Stripe after last night and this morning." I'll have the same, I said.

Girl, no they didn't play that song, Rita Marley's Feelin' High is rocking the speakers. I remember singing along with that while watching my cousin Robert smoking a joint at our neighbor's Basement party. Just smelling that made me high enough to get a good buzz as if I were smoking myself. The waiter comes back with our drinks and asks if we're ready to order? I'll have the; Mackerel, Ackee, Callaloo and dumpling says Diamond. I'll have the Liver with plenty of onions, Callaloo and plantains.

Where did you find this place it's beautiful? I found it amongst my travels and had to find a restroom stop and this was it, she says. What do you have on your agenda today, Ava? Well, tonight is the actual class reunion which is held at the ballroom of the hotel I'm staying at, why what are you doing? I want to do you so you'll have something to think about when you go home Diamond said. I told her to watch what she says and how she looks because this isn't the place to draw any attention towards us.

Would you stay at the hotel with me until I leave for California? Nearly jumping out of her skin she flashes a smile saying" Yes, I would love to. This will give us a sneak preview of us living together." Oh! You've got this all figured out don't you I said. Our food arrives smelling good, I slice a piece of the liver checking for its tenderness and it's like butta. How's your Mackerel, I asked. Before I knew it she is shoving a piece in my mouth, perfectly seasoned I couldn't help but moan in awe. Um, excuse me you never said when you were leaving, Ava. I thought I told you I leave day after tomorrow at 8:50pm.

Her mood changed quickly from being enthusiastic to solemn. She didn't say anything else while eating. I had the waiter pack up our plates in a to-go box and I paid the bill. We left the restaurant headed to the beach so we can talk. Finally a word was spoken," Do you have to go back so soon? She asked. Honey, I have to get back to work, my company is about to merge with Abbott Brindle Pharmaceuticals and I must be there.

When will I see you again, Ava?

I'm not sure, but how about I buy you a ticket today for you to come to California, put you in a hotel close by my job that way I can see you anytime. I saw a big smile appear on Diamond's face then she asked are you serious? You will do that for us, I mean me?"

I love you, Ava and these few hours have been just marvelous, and to just have a sample will be a tease. I became numb and speechless because at that time I was feeling like I was single all over again, like Philip who? I finally got the words out my mouth," Diamond, I love you too." Oh! Shit what did I just do? Then my inner ego interferes and puts its two-cent in saying, "Damn that when you're good you're good, and fuck that Philip dude he's just like a hype man to you. Get yo' girl, your true love and be happy. Bitch you ain't no cat with nine lives, you only live once."

We get to a more secluded section of the beach and park to continue to talk about if there will be a future and where will it take place, Florida or California. Diamond what you expect from me if we're to pick up from 30 years ago because we're not teenagers anymore and we have developed different personality's etcetera. Ava, I only request that you respect me, love me, keep an open line of communication and be honest to me. Oh! Two more things love me the way you do no less but more and keep the sex coming, she said. Well, those don't sound like difficult demands. I expect the same from you and to reciprocate on the love making once you've gotten the hang of what turns you on and what turns me on more.

Do you realize if I decide to be with you, it will take some time before the divorce is final? Philip will attempt to take a large percentage for alimony. Yes, and I'll wait because I've missed you all these years and I can't be without you again, Ava.

Have you ever loved so much that it hurts? Love so much that it makes you cry even when you're happy? Well, that's how I've felt these past 30 years without you, Diamond. You never left my thoughts but I suppressed my memories to survive my marriage to Philip.

Would you like to relocate to California, stay in Florida or both places, I asked of Diamond. She responds" Mmm,

They're both similar in climate so both places. I think you'll be comfortable in my home, sunshine. Maybe this is premature but I'm excited about a future with Diamond. Look, a parasailing stand let's go try that, I said. Diamond says, "I don't think so." Not even if I am side by side with you, I asked. That will be the only way, Ava. Okay let's go so we ran to the stand to get in line.

The instructor asks us if this is our first time. Simultaneously we both responded," Yes, how can you tell?" He straps us both in a harness, gives us instructions and directs us to the water, where a boat is hooked up for us. One, two, three, four, five, and six why are you counting Ava she asked. Didn't he say count to eight and it's up, up and away? Before Diamond got a chance to answer we were up, up and away all right. Hey, this isn't so bad I said as I look at the roofs of some hotels, condos and stores on the beach. Diamond hadn't said a word because her eyes were clinched tightly closed. Open your eyes and look I told her, it's not bad at all.

The parasail was $25.00 per person for 30 minutes, which was worth every dollar. While we were coming in for a landing I noticed a nice cozy spot on the rocks that sat high, above the public eye to sit, chat, touch and smooch. In my mind I had visions of a nice lay out of tapered candles stuck in the rocks, two glasses of wine accompanied with portable CD player. I smile while in my private thoughts, all I hear is "Earth to Ava" and fingers snapping. I am awakened from my trance, yes, I'm sorry about that, Diamond. She asks, "Where did you go?" You will see soon enough. I replied. My inner ego enters the picture again with its two cents,

“That’s my girl, go after what you want. She won’t resist you after this shit you’ve got planned.” The ego continues to babble on by saying “Don’t forget the master of ceremony, Will Downing you’ll be fucking on them rocks tonight after hearing your favorite songs, “She and The Nearest of you.”

With no warning, I yell out “you damn straight” and I look at Diamond like a cat that swallowed a canary. What do you have up your sleeves, Ava she asked in a nervous tone? Don’t worry about it, after the reunion I’ll pick you up from the room and we’ll go for a ride to my surprise. Speaking of which, I need to go to the mall for a few things let’s go to the mall, pulling Diamond by the hand. We arrive at the Galleria Mall in Ft. Lauderdale; in which we had to split from each other in order to get the things on my shopping list, therefore I told her to go into Victoria Secret’s to get her anything she wanted to wear tonight and tomorrow handing her $300.00 cash. She ran off like a kid in a candy store.

I in turn went into my candy store, FYE’s music store to find Will Downing’s albums; A Dream Fulfilled and The Greatest Hits. Then it’s off to Yankee Candle to get some tapered candles. I found some scented ones, so I got a box of twelve then off to find a portable CD player and batteries. I see Diamond at the register in Victoria’s Secret so that’s my cue to hurry out to the lobby. Did you find everything you needed, Ava she asked? I need two things batteries and a CD player, Oh I have one in the car you can use mine, she says. Great, I said. We then make our way back to the car to head back to West Palm Beach.

...The Passion Continues

On the ride back to the room, Diamond turns the radio to an underground station where they play nothing but Reggae music. They were jamming songs by; Buju Banton, Sean Paul, Carlene Davis, Nadine Sutherland and Beres Hammond. I told Diamond that it was something about Jamaican accents that just makes me wet my panties and why did I say that, she began speaking Patois. She was so good that I thought we picked up a hitchhiker. She says, Looka ear pickney ta-nite ya belong ta I. I tink dat der punany gwan get beatin wit mi tongue. I was tickled because as minimal as it was she was willing to do anything to make me happy. Alright don't get me excited or I'll make you talk to me like that all night long.

Okay what did you buy in Victoria's Secret, Diamond? I brought two Chemises; one in Canary yellow, one in Lavender, a few thongs in assorted colors and some scented oils. I can't wait to see you in all of them, I said. Baby, why did you need to buy all those things she asked? You shall see just be patient my dear I said in my evil voice. As we enjoyed the breeze of the night air I reached over to rub her thighs while she grips the steering wheel tighter. What are you doing, Ava I can't concentrate while you do that. To taunt and tease her more I slide my hand up her skirt to stroke her fat pussy, easing a finger at a time under her underwear until I feel the warm wetness running down my finger. I don't think you will make it to the festivities tonight at this rate baby, she says as she squirms trying to contain her composure while at a red light next to other cars. Diamond, you hadn't said nothing but a thing let's turn this car around and we'll go on to my surprise. She spins out making a U-Turn right in front the car in the next lane pulling into a car dealership's lot for me to take over driving.

I head back to the spot on the beach I saw from Parasailing but stop off to pick-up a bite to eat to complete my surprise. We grabbed some finger foods from the local restaurant on Las Olas. I blindfolded Diamond as we approach the spot, therefore I can set up the rocks for our evening of passion. I spread a blanket on the rock; stick the tapered candlesticks in holes that would hold them, placed the CD player in a cavity deep enough to cradle it. Then I go to the car and get Diamond leading her still blindfolded slowly up the side of the rock hill. I pull off the blindfold as we reached the top; then I light the candles which illuminated in an open heart shape, then pressed play on the player to have the balladeer Will Downing croon, "She." Diamond begins to get teary-eyed and says, "I love you, and Ava this is the nicest thing I've ever seen."

We sit on the rocks and begin to feed each other shrimp kabobs looking into each other's eyes ever so passionately that we didn't finish our food. I move closer to her to place my arms around her, captivated by the candlelight bouncing off those beautiful eyes, I lean in to her and we kiss passionately. Diamond then melts in my arms and one passionate kiss led to awkward lovemaking that will never be forgotten by either of us for we have scars to look back on and reminisce. I can't believe my trip is almost over, though this won't be the last time I see Diamond I'm already feeling that emptiness inside. I never thought I would ever be in her arms again let alone with any woman for that matter. All these years I've tucked my past in between my legs that I didn't know what I was really missing was true love.

We returned to the hotel hours later to shower and turn in for the night. The hotel concierge says, "Good evening Mrs. Mitchell I have messages held for you" and he passes me three slips of papers; one message from Philip saying he'll pick me up from the usual spot at the airport and two from the school reunion committee asking if I am still coming to the cruise. In my mind I'm saying to myself, I've already had the best cruise and reunion in my life and won't wait another 30 years to do it again.

...3...

Back in California

Meanwhile Ava has returned to California from her trip to West Palm Beach, Florida. Philip greeted her at the airport surprising her with a beautiful tropical floral arrangement. Hi, Baby how was your trip, um Ava, where is my hug? Philip says as he hands her the flowers to take her luggage. I'm sorry, honey I must have been in La-La land you know how that is you do it all the time. My trip was wonderful, I saw a lot of faces I didn't think I'd see. Like who? Hun, he asked. Do you remember that singer Kenny Barrington who sang, Miss Kissing You back in the 1980's? He was there with a classmate of mine, who had the reputation of being a Gold-Digger back then. I guess Kayne West knew her too I said jokingly to get the attention off of me. My mind kept wandering back and forth to Diamond and our love making last night, which was better than the first night.

Philip, are my fish still alive? I asked changing the subject again. Yes, the fish are fine is that all you care about are those fish he said angrily. No, that's not all I care about but you know how much money I spent on those fish and you pitched a bitch fit about it. Yeah Okay, tell me more about your trip he says. I saw my childhood friend who is planning to come out in two weeks. I went window-shopping because I didn't want to carry extra baggage, went to lunch at this nice Jamaican Restaurant called Café Calypso the usual stuff you do on vacation, relaxed.

What you did while I was gone, I asked. Not too much; I worked, fixed the lock on the laundry room door, cut the grass, hung out with Bernard and Jeff. I cooked your favorite dish for dinner so you don't have to worry about that tonight. Aww! You are so sweet, I appreciate that, I just want to take a bath and relax anyway I said. We arrive at 2612 Mulberry Lane, home sweet home. I'll be downstairs after my bath Philip, I yelled from the top of the stairs. Ok! Take your time he responds. I am so tempted to call Diamond that I am pacing the floor but I'll be good and wait until I get to the office although I will email her later on.

Ring. Damn, that's my cell phone, it's probably Janice anyway I'll call her later too. I need to enjoy this hot bubble bath right now, it's me time, and everyone else has to wait. Philip's voice comes over the intercom, "Honey, would you like a glass of wine while you simmer in that tub?" Yes, that would be nice, make it Pino Grigio white please I responded. He came in with the long stemmed glass of wine, he kisses me on the forehead and says, "You were really missed." Thank you sweetie and you were missed too. What a big lie, because I didn't think twice about him after seeing Diamond, I knew this was going to happen.

I have to really count my blessings finding a man like Philip, he's very attentive, handy, and non-abusive and he's even okay in the bedroom. How can I let that go for Diamond who I haven't seen in 30 years but still have such an adoration for after all this time. Diamond and I seem to have picked up where we left off at when we last saw each other when I was eighteen and she was sixteen years old. As if we didn't skip a beat! Ava, what have you gotten yourself into this time? I ask myself but my ego answers "You know you've always wanted her so you got the true love of your life. Yeah the old guy is good to you but do you glow with him as you do with her?

Damn, ego you're right. I don't glow like that with him; she is my true love, ugh! You've done it again. Do I go with my heart to be with Diamond or do I stay with my husband? I need to know something before I see Diamond because I know she will ask. Let me get something to eat and spend some time with Philip before he gets suspicious. Hey hun, whew! I feel much better thanks again for cooking dinner. What's on the television tonight or are we watching a video? I asked. Well, we have a choice of watching a rerun of Girlfriends on UPN or your favorite the inside of your eyelids since you always fall asleep watching T.V. he said. I'm so sorry Philip you're right maybe I should just turn-in tonight and start fresh tomorrow. Good Night. Okay, I'll be up soon sweetheart and he kisses me again on the forehead. Oh! Lord he's never kissed me so much and this forehead shit is played out like Vinyl records.

Ring, Ring. "Hello, Philip this is Janice is my girl home?" Hey Janice, she came home exhausted so she's asleep. I'll tell her you called in the morning. Hey how's your cousin Margo, Janice?" Philip asked. That clown is alright I guess, I haven't really spoken to her lately, why you like my cousin? Janice responded. Philip chuckled and said" she's cool peeps that's all." Yeah! That's all it better be or my girl will kick your ass. Now you know I wouldn't do that to my girl, Ava." Alright, I'll talk to you later, Janice. Good night, Philip she says. Philip then turns off the TV to turn-in himself. He approaches the top of the stairs to only hear Ava moaning in her sleep. He nudges her after listening for a while to see if the sounds change or she begins to talk in her sleep. Baby, are you alright? You're moaning in your sleep, I guess I was just having a bad dream that's all, thanks Philip.

Excuse me hun, bathroom time. Oh! Shit I was dreaming about a sexual encounter with Diamond and I was moaning, I need to be careful or just clear my mind before bed. Seeing the bright lights of the beautiful Los Angeles Skyline from the bathroom window has awakened me. So I think I'll go to my downstairs office, grab my laptop, and check my email from work until I fall off to sleep. I received an email in regards to the merger meeting and it looks like they agreed to the proposal between my company and the stockholders, wonderful. The merger is set for September 22, 2012. Yes!!!! I can retire before the age of fifty, hell I can even buy a home in West Palm Beach and a private jet to be closer to Diamond if I wanted.

That was enough good news to make up my mind whether I want to stay with Philip or settle down with my Diamond. I am sure Diamond would love that, and then I can spoil her the way she deserves. Just thinking about her makes me want her more and more. I love the way we fit together like a puzzle when we're spooning and making love. It's nothing like being a contortionist when there are two different heights and you're trying to get positioned comfortably and whoever said "Everybody is the same height lying down" is sadly mistaken. How is someone who's 6'3" and someone who's 5'4" the same at any point in time?

Let's see what other kind of good news we can find in my e-mail. I am bursting at the seams! I got to call Diamond, 561-555-0006 it's ringing. Hi sunshine, I said as she answers the phone in a sleepy tone. She perked right up like the sunrise when she heard my voice. Hi honey, I miss you already she says. Did I wake you from your beauty rest? I asked. Baby, you can wake me up anytime. Why are you up at 2 O'clock in the morning? She asked. I told her it started off as a trip to the bathroom but once I opened my eyes and saw all the lights from our skyline I was wide-awake. So now I am checking my e-mail and I had some good news, my company has bought another pharmaceutical company which will put me in the position for early retirement! Oh congratulations big shot, she replied with an excitement that I could feel through the phone.

Thank you baby! You know this means I can be closer to you or vice versa? I'm thinking of maybe purchasing a West Palm Beach home, a jet, and dumping my husband. All I heard was a loud scream "Get the fuck out, are you serious. Is that really what you're considering doing?" she asked. Diamond, these past few days I spent with you has been like a new beginning of life for me. Maybe that's what I need and to stop being someone I'm not just for White Corporate America to accept this African American successful woman. I want to be happy one hundred percent of the time not seventy percent of the time. One day Philip will get suspicious because since I've been home I forgot to kiss him at the airport, I hadn't spent too much time with him and he had to ask how was my trip instead of me was just telling him.

I did tell him you were coming in two weeks though to get it out in the air. He even offered you to stay at my house but I told him you already had these arrangements long before I got to Florida. I have to ease things on him and to have you in the house and not be able to make love to you, sleep with you, will be strenuous on me. That's why I reserved a room for you at the Biltmore Hotel down the street from my office, where I have easy access to you at any point of the day or night. I do tend to stay at work overnight in my office sometimes so I wouldn't be doing anything out of my norm. I really hate the fact that I would be sneaking around while you're here but you have to at least come to the house to have dinner with us. Diamond; please control the lustful looks and no footsies under the table either, so I am asking you to be good. Don't worry it's you I really want to be with I am sure of that now.

Well, its 4:55AM and Philip is getting up in twenty minutes so I'll talk to you later sunshine. "Ava, I love you, and I am looking forward to seeing you again." Same here Diamond. As I hang up Philip is standing in the doorway and asks "who are you talking to this time of the morning? " I was checking my messages at work and I forwarded it to Martha with additional information I needed her to follow up on Monday morning. Hoping he didn't hear the conversation, I ask jokingly, did you think I was talking to my other man?" He says "No, I just thought that nut Janice called you back because she called while you were asleep." Oh boy she's going to tear another hole in my ass for not calling her when I got home. I told her you were tired so you went to sleep, he says in my defense. That's one thing I liked about him he's always ahead of me when I don't want to be bothered by some phone calls. Philip, do you think we can have lunch together today at our favorite spot? I ask to make up for my not spending time with him when I got home. He says, "As long as we can stop by Cold Stone Creamery for desert." It's a deal I'll meet you at the restaurant at 1:30pm as I kiss him good-bye.

Climbing the stairs to return to my bed I noticed I left my cell phone in my office downstairs, just as I turn around to go pick it up, Ring, Ring, damn, just my luck it's ringing and I'm sleepy! Phil must have forgotten something. It stops ringing before I get to it and its Janice because she knows I sometimes wake up with Phil before he goes to work. I may as well get this over with so let me call her back. Hey, Janice" I am so sorry I didn't call you last night I was tired. So did you enjoy your trip? She asks. Yes, I enjoyed my get away and the reunion. Phil told me he cooked dinner for you did you enjoy it? I didn't eat much but yes it was nice of him, I said. What's wrong, bitch? You don't sound right nor were you still asleep? Talk to ya girl, She asked. Yes, I was asleep I said.

Uh oh, the damn Poe-Poe has sniffed out my guilt. I'm ok in fact I have been up since 2 O'clock don't ask why but I'm fine, Janice. Tell that to somebody that doesn't know you, Ava. No, honestly I am ok, I assured, maybe I am still a little jet-lagged let's try this conversation again later on today, ok Janice? I'll let you off the hook this time go back to sleep I'll call you later. That girl can smell a skunk without being outside she's so hungry for gossip and Lord knows I'm not the one to provide it to her. Ah! Back in bed, I'll turn off all phones so I can get some sleep. My body literally melted into the Goose Down Duvet cover the moment I laid down. I immediately fell off into a slumberous sleep, so deep that I almost over slept missing my lunch date with Philip.

It's just after 12 o'clock, I rush to get ready for my luncheon with Philip when my cell phone vibrates and dances on the nightstand, its Diamond. I answered it, telling her I will call her back when I get in the car. In a rush I can't find my car keys so I call Philip to ask him where the keys are, by this time it's already 1 O'clock. Philip, have you seen my car keys? Oh! You didn't get my message off the house answering machine. I called once I discovered they were in my pocket and cancelled our lunch date due to an extended meeting. I explained to Philip I had the ringer turned off so I could get some sleep. Then I called Janice to bring me my spare car key. I get Janice's voice mail; therefore I had to leave a message. "Janice, this is Ava I need you to bring me my spare car key Philip took it by mistake and I need to do some errands."

I called the restaurant to place an order for me to take to Philip's job as a surprise. Hello, Ruby this is Ava Mitchell how have you been? I've been better than an old dog these days, what can I get you today, Ava? Let me have the usual for me and for Philip let me have the BBQ Rib special. That man hungry again, Ruby says. I was confused so I asked "Ruby, What do you mean by that?" Well, Ava you know I don't get into nobody's business or start rumors but Philip was here for a late breakfast with a nice young lady by the name of Margo. Mmmm? I know a Margo, she doesn't live here, but I'm going to take a shot at this, Ruby by chance did this Margo person have a birthmark on her left cheek in the shape of Louisiana? Ruby said laughing, "Yes, now that you mention it. Oh! So you know this nice young lady." I told Ruby this is our secret and told her I'll pick up my order at 1:30. Ok what the fuck is going on here; let's see it's not my birthday or our anniversary and I didn't tell him about the merger, so, what could this be about. What's taking Janice so long to get back with me? Knock, Knock. Who is it I asked? It's your Chauffeur. Who do you think it is? It's Janice you rang mistress, laughing.

Hey girl, thanks you're a god-send come on in, Janice. Whoa! Did you know your fish laid some eggs on the glass wall, Ava? I hadn't noticed that last night, awww I'm going to be a mother of some sort of fish. How's your family in Kentucky doing, Janice? Well the last time I heard all is fine Charles, Margo and punk is supposed to be in town for a church trip to Disneyland in August. Other than that they are fine she says. Well, I got to get back to work, don't think you're getting off the hook from our conversation. Love you, Heffa talk to you later. Ok its June so why is Margo here and not telling her cousin who was practically raised by her. I hopped in my car to get to Ruby's to surprise Philip with lunch. Uh Oh, DJ Lalah is playing my jam on the radio. I crank it up and start singing along not realizing how physical I was getting and this fine guy in the car next to me says, "That must be real good to you." I blushed and said "It's the Isley Brothers, of course it's good to me."

I pull up in the parking lot of Ruby's but I park on the back street of the parking lot to avoid being noticed if Philip should be in the streets. Hey! Ava, someone yells from the kitchen. I am bending down to look for the person who was calling me. Then I get this big hug and it's Ruby. Since when do you work in the kitchen I asked Ruby? I am short a cook for a few hours Tony's wife went into labor and I am waiting on Lionel, she explained. Did I cause a problem telling you about this mystery woman, Ava she asked? No she's a family friend but still it will be our secret maybe they're planning a surprise for me, I said. Oh! That's nice Ruby said. Alright then Ruby I'll talk to you later.

I sprinted to my car so I can see the look on Philip's face as I show up un-announced. As I enter the building the Receptionist isn't there so that's my opportunity to not be seen and Philip be notified of my arrival. As I jet to the elevator I see his boss and he says "Is that my lunch you're bringing me?" How are you this wonderful day Mr. Cornelius? I said. Oh! I'm blessed and highly favored he responded. I knew by that comment he was getting ready to go on the religious role, while at the same time he's fornicating in his mind.

I walk into Philip's office and he's not there so I leave the lunch with a note saying I hope you enjoy. As I walk through the hallway I gaze into the park at the children playing on the swings then I cruise the rest of the park only to see Philip and Margo hugged up under the bridge. I rush downstairs to grab my camera from the car to take pictures because I can use this to start my divorce proceedings and go on with my life with Diamond.

I make it to the car and grab the camera and walk to the park from the back of the bridge's entrance to go un-noticed. I take three pictures, one of them kissing ever so passionately, my blood begins to boil but I catch myself and calm myself down. I suddenly here my inner ego whisper in my ear "Just snap the fucking pictures and leave. You know this evidence will support you in the long run." "Okay, you're right, just breathe in and out deep," I said. I ran back to my car then continued on my way. I forgot to call Diamond, she'll probably think I don't keep my word, therefore let me call her now. Hey, Baby a sweet voice on the other end says. You better stop assuming it's me when you see my number pop up on that Caller-ID it could've been Philip. You're so right but now that I know it's you "Hi baby. I miss you so much" she whimpered.

I just got finished playing I-Spy on my husband. What do you mean, Ava? I call myself surprising him with lunch since he had a long meeting today but the surprise was on my ass. I called a restaurant to order lunch and the owner Ruby says to me that Philip was there with some nice young lady named Margo.

This Margo is my best friend Janice's cousin who raised her and on the sly I asked Janice how was she and she volunteered information of her expected arrival in August. I saw them in the park cuddled up together and kissing under a bridge, so I took pictures. Now my dear you have to know exactly where your heart is because I don't want to put myself out there to be hurt once I change my whole world. Diamond replies with an elated sigh of rejoice in her voice, "I love you very much and I don't need another 30 years to figure that out, therefore I am willing to combine my world with yours to create one wonderful universe. This is it then, I will call my attorney to get things rolling first thing tomorrow.

...4...

The Countdown

Okay, who sent the flowers this is a trap if ever I saw one. If Philip didn't send them he'll blow his lid then I'll be forced to expose what I know about his lunch date. I got this; I got this I said to myself. Let me call Diamond to feel the conversation to see if they came from her first.

I start scrambling around looking for my travel agent's cell number to make the arrangements and in come Philip. Hello, Honey I am home, he yells. I'm upstairs I'll be right down I said. As I find it, and begin to dial Phil comes in my office to inquire who gave me flowers. I told him I'd tell him when I get off the phone. Hello Ricardo this is Mrs. Mitchell calling to make some changes on those travel arrangements. Hey Mrs. Thang, how was your trip to Florida he asked. Wonderful, I need those tickets for Diamond LaRue to be changed to tonight standby flight and the hotel reservations changed for tonight also, can that be arranged Ricardo? Mrs. Mitchell of course that can be arranged and I'll even waive the service charge for changes since you're my favorite client.

Awww! Ricardo I'll owe you one, what I can do for you, I asked. Laughing he responds I'll get back to you on that, Mrs. Mitchell he says and here is your confirmation number 15656SPG195; flight 265 departing out of West Palm Beach International at 10:55pm scheduled to arrive into Chicago O'Hare Airport at 12:20am connecting flight 925 leaves for LAX Airport arriving at 1:55am and the hotel has been notified of changes with a room upgrade to Executive suite with Jacuzzi. Will that be all Mrs. Thang he asks?

Ricardo, when was your last vacation I asked. To be honest Mrs. Mitchell I don't recall when I had a real vacation just a couple of days off and stayed home to do nothing he says. I'll tell you what check with your supervisor for a week off and I'll fly you and your companion out to LA and I'll show you around to the hot spots. LA! Are you serious Mrs. Thang you're offering to pay my way to LA, and I can bring my companion? Luis will be so happy he says. Who's Luis, your boss I asked. No he's my companion he replied. Knowing all along he was a family member you just have to play it off. Oh! Ok that's cool take my cell phone and let me know when you're ready I'll take care of you as you've done for me the past twelve years.

Phil, where are you honey I yelled out as I walk the corridor of the second floor. I'm in the restroom he says. I'll be downstairs when you get out, okay. I am so excited that I can't contain myself from excessive smiling. Fast paced walking Phil hits the stairs to interrogate me in regards to the flowers. So you have another admirer, Ava he asks. Now you know there is enough of me to go around sweetheart, I responded sarcastically. To be honest, I'm not sure who sent them to me did you send them? Um! No I didn't I wish I did thou' it's a beautiful gesture he says. I throw around ideas that maybe it's someone from the office welcoming me back home or a client.

I am going to the office tonight to start arranging my work for the rest of the week; dinner will be delivered by Mama Lucia's I've had a full day already and I didn't get a chance to start dinner. Okay, I may go shoot some hoops with the boys tonight so I'll be home late myself, he says. In my head I'm thinking sure you're going to play ball, more like getting your balls played with. I didn't argue or seem upset knowing Margo is in town while I go get Diamond; I go upstairs to get my briefcase organized.

Ding Dong. Phil get that its Mama Lucia's I already pre-paid them just tip them okay? I said yelling from upstairs. I got it honey, Mmmm it's smells good this must be my favorite dish, Stromboli he says. I smile and mumble "You better believe I'm going to continue to make you happy while you think I'm blind to your plot of deceit, but you'll never suspect me and mine." Baby, aren't you going to eat before you go he says. Yes, I'll be right down. Am I forgetting anything, I ask myself I guess I've got everything. Phil, would you be so kind as to put my Stromboli in the oven on medium and I'll be down in ten minutes. Okay, but I'll probably be gone by the time you get down here Bernard just paged me, so, I'll be heading to the hoops. That's okay I'll make sure I'm down before it burns, have fun sweetie.

I search my drawer for my favorite lingerie to bring along for enticing. I brought this purple lace one piece with a plunging neckline to reveal my robust cleavage with a crotch split. I have never had the opportunity to wear it for any special occasion. I truly think this warrants a special enough occasion to bring it out of hiding, hell Phil doesn't even know it exists. Okay let me go eat and watch a little Television and bask in the moment, knowing in two hours and forty-five minutes my sweetie will be landing in my arms. Let me call my girl Janice to see what she's been up to these past few days and pull information out of her about Margo. Hey, I thought you kicked me to the curb since I hadn't heard from you all day, Janice says before her usual phone greeting. Now why would I do that I said. I am calling you now because I have some free time until I head out, so you can cut me some slack on your attitude.

Hey, I'm glad you called though I need a pain killer for my toothache until I get to the dentist on Friday. Now you know I can't give you any narcotics you're already psychotic but I can give you some Advil or Tylenol Extra Strength which will be better for you anyway. Janice, you're always looking for a hook-up one day you're going to get your hook-to land you in a cold cell with somebody big then you'll be their bitch holding onto their pocket liner following them all around the courtyard. That's bullshit I'll never be anybody's bitch let alone a female's property, she says in a loud tone. Don't be so sure of what life can throw your way.

Anyway, what's going on in your life Janice? You would not believe this but I think I'm in love but he doesn't know it yet. What do you mean he doesn't know yet? Did you talk to him and tell him you like him, did you two go out? What's the scoop, Janice? I saw this guy in the mall at one of those Kiosk buying vitamins and I dropped my clipboard and we bent down to pick it up at the same time, our eyes met and he said "I'll get that for you beautiful" in his baritone voice.

Ava, he had gray eyes; stood 6'5", maybe 235 lbs., sporting a wife beater Tee and legs to climb like a tree. I'm sorry Janice but what makes you think you'll see this hunk again?

Girl, I followed him and he works at your favorite store and I overheard a clerk ask if he can close the store tomorrow night. Ava, you have to come with me tomorrow so we can play it off. Janice, I can't but I'll do better I'll get my girl Chanel to give me the scoop on him and I'll get back to you. Is that a promise, Ava? I got your back on this don't worry. Janice, I got to run we will talk tomorrow okay as I dashed out to get to the airport. Okay, later gator she says. Just before I dashed out I left Phil a note on the pillow saying…

It's a possibility I'd be staying at my office depending on my work load if things change I'll call you…
Love Ava

...Reuniting

I hop into the car and hit the boulevard heading towards LAX, which is a twenty-minute ride. The closer I got the more excited I got so to calm my nerves I pop in a Jazz compilation CD with Nancy Wilson, Al Jarreau, Kim Waters, Nenna Freelon and many other great artists who always seem to get me to relax. I took a detour to the 24hour florist shop to pick up a bouquet of flowers, which is located at the entrance of the airport before you get into the mess of the heavy traffic. I arrive in the parking lot all of a sudden feeling nervous as if it's my first date. I guess because I know that for once in my life I can feel 100% happiness and it be genuine without any compromising to hinder the joy.

I see Diamond as I walk to the luggage carousel, trying to go around behind her to surprise her but she turns around too soon and spots me. She runs to me with the biggest smile; twinkling eyes and I greeted her with tears in my eyes. Diamond says, as she wipes my tears away, "why are you crying, baby?" You just don't know how happy I am inside and out when I am with you. As we headed to the car I asked how her flight was and did she want to stop and eat? She said the flight was good very little turbulence and what I do want is to hear why you're crying, Ava.

Let me explain something to you Dee, do you remember your favorite childhood toy that got broken or lost? Yes, I had a doll named Ms. Beasley and she went everywhere I went and I lost her when I went to Belize with my grandmother, Diamond replied. I am sure you wanted another one to replace her didn't you, I asked. They weren't making those dolls anymore but yes I wanted another one and no exceptions either my parents brought me all kinds of dolls to pacify me for my loss. I wanted what I wanted because I was daddy's little girl, Diamond said. Exactly my point you didn't want any imitations of Ms. Beasley. When we were younger and had our innocent fling it made such an impact on me that I associated the feeling I experienced as love, which felt so good that I wanted to feel that way again after we parted. I searched for someone with same qualities as you from your height, your smile, sensitivity and sense of humor but I ended up with abusive people who didn't love me or who were just out to put another notch on their belts with some other agendas.

Therefore, all these years I was looking for your love for me in others and it just wasn't the same even with Philip. Ava, it's going to be alright I'm back in your life forever if you'll have me, providing your circumstance at home changes. Quarter sized drops danced on the windshield as we approached the hotels valet. Wait a minute! She says. "Tony Toni Tone sang that song about it never rains in Southern California." Girl, don't believe everything you hear except for what comes from my lips. I self-parked in the garage of the hotel and we're met by a bellhop who greets me with an unexpected hug and says" Mrs. Mitchell you are truly an inspiration to my children and the community, I thank you! And he takes the bags.

Dee says, "Damn did you pay him to say that or are you just big timing like that? Laughing I respond 'No, I didn't pay him nor was I expecting him to greet me like that. He over hears the conversation and comments. Excuse me, he says "I take it you do not live here or you would know what this young lady has done for the community and the youth." Diamond responds in a surprised tone, No I don't live here then turns to look at me wide-eyed and says, "I'm so proud of you."

The Concierge greets us "Welcome to the Biltmore Mrs. Mitchell and guest." Simultaneously Dee and I respond "Thank You!" Jorge!!! The clerk from behind the desk yells "Can you please escort Mrs. Mitchell and her guest to PH2053? Jorge shuffled over to us and escorts us to two bright and shiny gold elevators and pushes the button for our floor.

I tipped Jorge as we entered our penthouse and locked the door behind him. Dee looks out the window to gaze at the skyline of Los Angeles. This is so beautiful she says. Are you ready to turn in and get ready for our day tomorrow, I asked of Diamond? Stretching and yawning she says, "Is jetlag written all over my face?"

...5...

The Separation Process

Six-Forty the sun rises over the city's skyline and soft lips pressed on my cheeks awakens me. Good morning my dear says Diamond, are you ready for breakfast she asks. What's on the menu, I ask with a devilish tone. Baby, I will be your meal and she spreads eagle over my face. I dare not turn down breakfast in bed. I pulled up the sheet as if it were my bib and commenced to eating the meal placed before me.

Nothing but silence for the first few seconds then all the gates flew open. I could not swallow fast enough before my face was doused again and again with love juices. I suddenly hear a knock on the door and a voice from the other side of the door says, "Can you please hold down the noise?" As embarrassing as it was I was quick on my feet, I responded with bass in my voice "Man, you must have left your pussy home" then I hear the door slam.

Diamond is still gyrating and feeling high from me cleaning my plate so to speak. Baby, she gasped, as she lays back on the bed panting, what are you trying to do to me? I am only trying to satisfy you sweetie, I said. I reached out to get my cell phone off the nightstand to call my attorney and start the filing procedures. Who are you calling, Hun? I told you I took some pictures of my husband kissing another woman the day after I returned home from the reunion. Dee literally stands up in the bed and says "Yes, does this mean you're mine now?" Diamond, I'll always be yours, but now I've got to work on making it official. I don't recall the whole story, tell me again what happened? Well, a brief synopsis, I was planning on having lunch with Phil the day after my return from Florida but he canceled the lunch due to a meeting plus he had my car keys. Janice came and brought my spare keys so I picked up his favorite dish from our favorite restaurant. When I was at his job I saw some kids playing in the park adjacent to his office, so I took a walk, while out there, I saw Phil's ass kissing another woman, but the restaurant owner had already told me he was there for lunch with another woman who fits the description of my friend Janice's Cousin Margo.

I pulled the pictures out of my briefcase to show Diamond and she looked at them so close and says "Damn he's handsome and she is U-G-L-Y." I couldn't do anything but laugh; well he can be with her now without a fight from me. I proceeded to call my attorney not realizing it wasn't even eight O'clock yet but this is important. The phone is ringing. Hello says the sleepy voice on the other end. Hi Cecil this is Ava. Is everything alright Mrs. Mitchell? He asks. Can we meet in the next three hours in your office, Cecil?

Sure anytime will do Mrs. Mitchell I'll see you then, hanging up the phone. Diamond, I will drop you off down the street at the Brazilian Spa to get a nice treatment while I meet with Cecil. Baby, you're going to spoil me, that isn't necessary, I'll stay here and go for a swim or work out in the gym, Dee says ever so softly. Are you sure that's what you want to do while I go to see Cecil, I asked. She replies "Baby you're going to make a very important step in your life which will change a lot, I am sure I can stay here until you return." I love you I said kissing her supple lips.

Let's go eat breakfast before I go to Cecil's office, I said as I grabbed Dee's hand leading her to the shower. Mmm, she says as the hot water ran down the front of her well-endowed breasts. We lather each other up with Lavender body wash and as the scent illuminates the air we again sexually enticed. I nibble on the nape of Dee's neck almost sending her into an uncontrollable frenzy. That shit just builds my ego to be able to turn on a woman so easily.

...Flashback to days of Ole'

I recall this older woman at my job when I was Twenty-Nine years old asking me to verify a rumor. I ask pertaining to what may I ask. Well, rumor has it that you like women, Vicky, says. Me, with my smart-ass mouth responded, "What the fuck do you mean, like women?" She stumbled over her words because she saw I was getting upset. In a stuttering voice she says "it it wwwas a ru-ru MOR." Later that week I went to a Gay fashion show sponsored by Center One for AIDS and who did I see in the show, Vicky! She sashayed in front and spotted me in the crowd and winked her eye at me.

She was looking hot as hell in that hot pink outfit though. Later that night we hooked up, had drinks and it was on in the back of my beat up Econoline van. Hell, I blamed it on the liquor just like the guys do. I've never seen a more sensitive person in my life than Vicky and you think a girl her size wouldn't be so flexible either. Wrong! I called her Queen Twister in the office as a personal inside joke. One day around the fax machine Vicky approached me and asked if we could hang out again after work. I kept making up excuses to not be available but she wore me down five months later.

Vicky and I met up at Club Sassafras on Wilshire Blvd. for happy hour and to see a local Jazz artist Joan Cartier perform. We must have closed the bar because the staff was pushing the broom across the floor. I was too drunk to drive home and Vicky drove me to her place. I woke up with my clothes all over the place starting from the living room all the way to the guest room where I woke up alone. I don't remember what happened in between my arrival and my waking up. This Six foot, Two-Hundred Seventy Three pound, dark chocolate skinned woman with the deepest dimples started to grow on me. We became fuck'buddies, until I met Phil in the office building next to our job. Vicky had a jealous streak that wasn't visible so it snuck up on a sista.

She would do drive-bys to my place and key his car, flatten our tires then at work give me attitude.

...Back to Reality

Dee and I end our shower and headed down to Snuffy's Buffet. Dee amazed at the beautiful layout from the; fruit, bread, veggies and meats. She proceeds scanning the fruit and picks up a strawberry dipped in chocolate and feeds it to me. Normally I wouldn't be caught being fed in public by someone other than myself but I couldn't resist those eyes. Dee has what I call chameleon eyes they change colors with mood and her clothes they're normally hazel but what gets me is when they're hazel with a hint of blue. I just melt when I think of her or when I'm near her. Feeling this way after thirty years for a person signifies real love and I know my filing for a divorce won't be a second thought or a hard process.

We finished breakfast then I walk her back to the suite to get my last kiss until I return from Cecil's office. Ava, she says and pauses but proceeds to say, "I truly love you and I hope I'm not forcing you to make this decision because I want to be with you?" Dee, honestly I knew all along that I got married for the wrong reasons. Had I not seen you and this still took place I would've had the ammunition for divorce. I'll see you in about two hours if I run late I will call you from the office.

My ego taps in again, "Girlfriend, you are on your way to get your eternal happiness. So why the long face, this is what you need in your life, Hell if not in your life in mine." A broad smile appears on my face as I glimpse the rear-view mirror. I turn on DJ Lalah's show to hear what she is playing, again a favorite of mine, Phyllis Hyman now that's a Diva in her own right. I've arrived to Cecil's office but I remain in the car to the end of the song.

The security guard spots me sitting in my car and nods at me, I wave back. I finish the song singing along and get out the car since the guard keeps watching me. I say "Good morning" as I approach him and he nods. People just aren't verbal anymore these days. I caught the elevator with another couple going up. What floor this blue-haired woman asks in her southern voice. Eighteenth please, I reply. The doors open to the ninth floor and she exits which houses the auditing office of the Internal Revenue Service. I cringe at that floor and pray I never have to stop there for anything. The guys who work there look so stuffy in their suit and ties, which will scare you into a sweat.

The elevators doors open to the eighteenth floor as I step out I see Cecil at the coffee machine through the glass doors. I entered the office and say "how's my favorite lawyer this morning?" Chuckling, he says, "Just fine Mrs. Mitchell to what do I owe the pleasure of our meeting today?" He closes the door behind us to his office and offers me a cup of coffee as I thumb through my briefcase. No thank you, handing him the pictures of Philip. Nearly burning his lip due to shock, "tell me that's not Philip" he says. Acting as if I'm in distress I responded, "Yes."

Oh! Mrs. Mitchell, I had no idea that you and Philip were having problems. Cecil, neither did I until I took these pictures last week. How did you find out about this affair, he asks. I was bringing him lunch as a surprise and I looked out the window of his office just gazing at the children playing and saw them under the bridge. What would you like to do at this point, Mrs. Mitchell? I want to start the filing proceedings, Cecil. I don't want anything from him and he can even keep the house if he can show financial statements he can afford the upkeep, property tax, and mortgage for the next eight months. If he's unable to then he can rent the home from me for Four Thousand dollars a month. Cecil is writing my requests down smiling then says, "Still being a humanitarian through to the bitter end." Don't get me wrong I love my husband and I'd hate to see him in a small one-bedroom apartment. This came to me as an embarrassment as if I wasn't the best wife I could be that he had to go out and cheat.

What makes it so bad is that the woman is my best friend's cousin, I said as Crocodile tears fill my eyes. Passing me the Kleenex box, I'm sorry extending his deepest regrets. When do you want me to present these documents, he asks. Right away, I exclaimed. I thank you for seeing me on such short notice Cecil as I make my way down the hall. Anytime, he says walking me to the elevators I'll be in touch Mrs. Mitchell.

While heading back to the car, I called Diamond just to tell her I'm on my way, but no answer… I forgot she went to the gym. I'll run up to my office to grab the messages off my desk along with any files I need to review for the merger. I see Markell coming in the building at the same time and we greet each other with a hug. Just as we enter my office

Markell asks, how was your trip Mrs. Mitchell? I was looking up at the hotel and smiling then I feel a tap on my shoulders, “Earth to Mrs. Mitchell” Markell says. I am so sorry were you speaking to me I ask. Laughing, he says your trip must have been off the chain because you’re in Never-Never land.

If you must know Markell my trip was fantastic and I can just relive it all over again in my mind. I won’t be in the office long so please hold my calls. Sure, anything else Mrs. Mitchell? He asked. No that will be all, thank you as I gaze out the window of my office.

…6…

No Turning Back Now

As I sat at my desk my cell phone rang and it was my attorney Cecil. “Hi Cecil, is everything okay?” I asked in a nervous tone. Everything is just fine Mrs. Mitchell; I was calling to make sure my favorite client is okay considering what was presented to me. Oh! That is so considerate of you, Cecil but I am okay, although I can’t say how I will feel when he is served the divorce papers.

If there’s anything I can do until then and thereafter just let me know Mrs. Mitchell, now you have a good afternoon. “Girlfriend, maybe you can play the field with the lawyer” says my ego. “Not now ego” I said. He’s single, good looking, got money and has a home on Fifteen acres of land. As I snap out of a daze shaking my head. I tell my ego,” Look ego, go rest yourself I don’t need any more on my plate.” I feel a slight vibration from my cell, glancing at the caller-ID I see its Diamond. Hey there sexy how was your workout? I ask. Just grueling she responds gasping for breath. I’m just leaving my office to run into those arms of yours. Diamond giggles let me shower first before you engage in my essence of funk. I’ll be there in two-minutes as I hang up the phone I see Philip is calling on the other end. Damn, I know Cecil is fast but he couldn’t have drawn up those papers that quickly. Should I answer the phone or ignore it? Ok, Ava get a hold of yourself bitch this is what you want. Be cool, I got yo’ back we ride or die bitches, says my ego.

What the hell, I’ll have to talk to him sooner or later “Hello?” I answered in a nervous tone anticipating a fight over the phone. Hello Mrs. Philip Mitchell would you like to meet me for dinner to make up for our missed lunch? Whew!! Gasping and clenching my chest he wasn't served the papers yet. Lord knows I wasn't ready to deal with this while Diamond was here. I'm sorry Philip I will be tied up with work and going over the merger details. Merger? What merger Ava, he says. Oh! I forgot to tell you that my company purchased IVRX Pharmaceuticals effective September 22; I guess everything clouded my mind and I forgot to tell you about it. He sits quietly on the other end before responding to my foul up. Then it was like a big bang of a drum "what do you mean you forgot to tell me, Ava?" We hadn't talked much since I've returned home so don't get on my case for failing to mention the merger. He says, "yeah what up with that too. It must be that motha fucka who sent those flowers taking up space in your head." He abruptly hangs up on my ass.

Let me get back to my baby who should be nice and fresh by now. As I stick my key into the door to our room I hear some romantic music playing. I ease open the door to see Diamond drying her hair and an opportunity to wrap my arms around her. Unexpectedly she takes a swing at me not realizing it was me and I get knocked upside the head with the dryer. Diamond screams apologetically I wasn't expecting you back so soon. I'm sorry let me get some ice baby as she pushes my hair back. Laughing I say "it's my fault I shouldn't have been sneaking in on you." Holding ice to my head like a good nurse Diamond gets teary-eyed. Now why are you crying? I'm okay I said, although it was hurting like crazy. How will you explain this to your husband and your co-workers she asks? Let me worry about that, sweetheart. Ava, did everything go okay at the attorney's office this morning? Yes, everything is set in motion I even had to act like I was really hurt by dropping a few tears. Would you believe I was nervous about answering my cell phone when Philip called me ten minutes ago?

I'll admit I thought I was going to shit bricks thinking that Cecil had the papers drawn up and delivered already. Philip called to ask me to have dinner with him and it slipped my mind that I didn't tell him about the Merger being accepted. Are you going to have dinner with him, Diamond asked with those puppy eyes, which were begging me to say no? I am where I want to be baby as I pulled her near me. The CD changer skips to the next CD only to play this new artist who was a local and he's got this satin voice that will make any woman dance out of her thong. Diamond says "Damn who is that?" I can't think of his name but I saw him at a charity function and I bought his CD. Let's see how your bruise is looking removing the ice pack from my head, our eyes met and Diamond plants a kiss on my forehead whispering "I love you, Ava." I reciprocated by whispering back "I love you too Diamond" while running my hand up her under chemise.

As my sometimes evil nemesis, my ego takes part in my delight. Now this is what I'm talking about, "shit we should've looked for her long time ago, Ava." Speaking out loud I blurt out "Not now dammit!" Diamond stops, and then looks at me "you bugging out." I'm trying to play it off by laughing. "No, I'm already ready to cum and I was telling my body not to explode yet." Damn, baby you're excited already she says. It doesn't take much when I'm near you, my love. Just as we are getting wrapped up even more in each other, the phone rings piercingly loud and startles me. Diamond says I'll get it.

Good Afternoon says the person on the other line, is this Ava Mitchell? Diamond pauses yes, one moment please...Ava... Diamond shouted in her bubbly voice. Honey, there's an Ace from a realty company on the phone asking for you. Is this an investor? Diamond inquires further. Giggling, why are you so nosey woman I'll get it in the kitchen? Mmm, ok be like that, keep secrets. Go get our stuff ready and I'll be up in a minute.

Hello this is Mrs. Mitchell speaking. Hello Mrs. Mitchell, Ace calling in reference to the completion of your new home in Fresno. I was wondering when you wanted to take a tour before all documents are final with the contractors. Yes, I would love to, what about this coming Tuesday say around, eleven in the morning. Ace ended the conversation by saying, that's perfect Mrs. Mitchell I'll meet you there, have a wonderful day. Oh! I will now Ava says hanging up the phone. Rushing upstairs to Diamond to see what type of fantasy room she has set up.

...Titillating Fantasy

I walk in the room to see her sitting at her laptop in bed and pointing to my office. As I entered my office I see my computer opened to Yahoo Messenger with a Post-it stuck on the monitor with instructions. I logged on and there was an offline message there saying: Let's create an online fantasy by typing whatever comes to mind to mesh with whatever I say. Here is the first line.

DIAMOND: I could tell she had a long day at work and all I wanted was to ease away some of the stress she was feeling...
AVA: So I come bearing two glasses of chilled wine in one hand... and in the other massage oils...
DIAMOND: I told her that tonight would be all about taking care of her every need... "Baby tonight, your wish is my command"…
AVA: Smiling ear to ear she leans back in the recliner sipping on Pinot Grigio... As I gently place my lips upon her breasts…
DIAMOND: She whispered to me how badly she wanted me and I began to gentle suck her nipples…
AVA: Mmm, the heat began and moans were in the air. She slowly spread open her legs and thrust her hips up and down in spiral motion...while calling my name to come closer to her warm creamy center…
DIAMOND: Straight to the point so as to not waste any time, we began to make love, wildly, passionately, pelvis to pelvis, panting with each thrust…

AVA: We strike the Crab pose of the Kama Sutra allowing the lips of our clits to touch and exchange creams only to make her scream with passion. Uh Uh Uh she pants as I strap on my appendage to only go deeper into her soul...
DIAMOND: With baited breath and penetrating moans she conjures a word, "Oh Baby" mmmm, yes baby, she claws at me, drawing me closer, inviting me deeper, I'm in tuned, I am picking up her quest, just as she is at the peak of passion...
AVA: She bends on one knee to swallow my essence... Trying to get every drop I hold the top of her head in such a position that I am forced to climax continuously. She begins to ride the mound of joy giving her pleasure after pleasure...
DIAMOND: Orgasms so intense she screams out in pleasure, I feel her at the core of me with hear scream, with every moan, I want to give more of myself to her, soon after her climax, she begins to weep. The experience took her to levels she hadn't before known...
AVA: Not getting enough of each other I flip her into the doggy position. I enter from the back ever so slow and gentle I enter her to give her what she longed for all these years. The deeper I go the louder the moans became intense. We felt each other's thrusting souls ready to blast off as the Challenger did. We released together with such passion Tears rolled down my face. I reach up to the sky asking "why did she have to wait so long to come to me."

Awww!!! This is some freaky shit… damn. Ava, where do you come up with these ideas? Diamond, you're an inspiration to all my juices that I secrete. I commence to moaning after that compliment. So intensely erotic that we couldn't help but act out our own virtual fantasy, hours later, sweating and panting for air, we curl up in each other's arms and before long Diamond drifts off into peaceful slumber; thoroughly exhausted yet deeply satisfied after that physical yet passionate role play. I lay awake for a bit, watching her rest, and then I got up to blow out the last of the candles when I saw a letter from her on the nightstand beside the bed.

...To Ava

...From Love...

You've shown me yourself and it is more than I could have ever imagined it would be. What could I have done to be so fortunate? "Some days I wake up and it takes me a second to remember that you're not a dream, you're real, and you're mine. I love you!"

...To Love...

After living without you for so long and finally experiencing your essence, I've come to realize how deeply deprived I've been. So beautiful and captivating, you have caused me to delve into the depths of everything that I thought I was in order to purge and make room for your magnificence and I am so glad I did. Because of you I laugh genuinely, sleep peacefully, live happily, and breathe easily. My heart pulsates excitedly when it feels you and I have come to understand and appreciate life in a way that heartache prevented me from doing in the past. I have become saturated with the gentle dew of you and I dare not remove myself from this outpouring.

...From Love to Love...

I am smitten by you... You character makes me proud, your fight encourages me, your passion arouses me, your laugh brings me joy, your drive reignites the flame within me that has been dormant for so long, your encouragement builds me up, your voice soothes me, your love has restored me, and my life has been forever changed for the better. I adore you...

For the rest of my days I will appreciate and cherish all that you mean to me. As cool sand beneath my feet, a gentle breeze caressing my skin and tender rain showers kiss me as passionately as you; your love has brought me an everlasting refreshing! I am yours and you are mine and no day will ever come that I will not look deeply through your eyes to your soul and from my core express how lucky I am to have you…

Heart n'Soul - I LOVE YOU

As I finish reading the letter, tears fill the wells of my eyes and I look over at her to see her sleeping so peacefully. I lean over to kiss her on the forehead; a smile appears on her face as if an angel had kissed her. I began to let the words flow from my pen to paper and this is what came to me.

...My Heart's Reply

My Dearest Diamond,

What can I do for you? What wish can I make come true? You've really been an awesome and very welcomed addition to my life. You found me broken and you have restored me. I lay myself bare before you today and invite you to take what you will. I'm yours! Come, kiss me, breathe the life of love into me, let me take you in, inhale your essence, utilize your breath as my vital substance. Such a sweet escape when I am near you, in your arms, loving you, feeling you, becoming one with you! Lying beside you, naked, our skin meeting, I feel whole, I feel comforted, your touch is healing.

What can I do for you? What wish can I make come true? You've loved me different than all the rest... no, you've loved me FOR REAL! I've never needed this much, never craved or ached this much. This past few days together has been utter bliss. If this world were mine, to create what I will, I would create a permanent place for you here beside me. Everything that would need to be handled would care for itself, while I care for, support, and enjoy you! LIFE with you!

What can I do for you? What wish can I make come true? I have to have you. Life without you is not an option for me. Come back ok? Don't stay away too long. Time away from you is always an adjustment, but this time, I don't want to adjust, I don't want to get used to home without you, I want you here with me, forever. The thought of coming home to you excites me, but more than that, it soothes me. Every night fear is erased with you beside me. I rest… babe… I rest…. Mmmm…

I need you, I want you, I adore you, I cherish you, I smell you, I taste you, I feel you, I breathe you, I SEE YOU, and it's beautiful…

Love Forever,
Ava

After writing to Diamond, I tried, though unsuccessfully, to sleep, but after laying there for quite some time I soon realized that sleep would elude me so I decided to make use of my time awake. As I turned to ease out of the bed to get some last minute notes out to my secretary, Diamond grabs my arms and whispers "where are you going"? I replied "going to get my laptop to send my secretary an email" and closed my reply with a kiss to Diamond's neck. "Come back soon," she manages to whimper out as she falls back to sleep.

Dear Gwen,
I am expecting a phone call from John Wu from China Exchange Tuesday but I won't be available. Please have Mr. Wu FedEx his proposal and I will review them over the next three days. On Wednesday, Cancel the meeting with Rite Aid representative and schedule a phone conference with Angelica Whittendale of Pathmark's Pharm-Co in Philadelphia. Additionally, I will not be available for any calls via my cell unless it's an absolute emergency. I will be back in the office on Thursday. Thank you!

Sincerely,
Ava Mitchell

I crawl back into bed and snuggle up closely to Diamond, and before long, I fall asleep with the biggest smile on my face. Diamond backs her butt into my stomach as spooning is her favorite sleep position. Only two more days before Diamond goes back home and I'm missing her already. We both fall into a deep slumber until my alarm blares loudly to wake me so I can go home to Phil.

Diamond turns over and says, "Nooooooo!" while pulling my arm around her waist as to hold me hostage. I whispered in her ear "we won't have to sneak around too much longer" while nibbling on her ear lobe which sends chills throughout her body. She shakes off the sensual chill and turns to me with this look of confusion on her face. I can see she wants to say something so bad but she holds her tongue. I get up, wash off and get dressed. Before leaving her I tell her, "I'll call you with our plans for today when Phil leaves the house."

As I approach the door to the hotel hallway, I stop and turn around to plant a wet kiss on Diamond. Just when it gets good, my phone rings and its Phil. I try to ignore the phone but he calls back to back. Naturally, my ego is awakened at the heightening of the passionate kiss and says "That fucker sure knows how to ruin a good thing." Ok, hun I must go before he decides to go to my office, I love you Diamond. "Aww! Shit somebody happy as pig in shit this morning." Good morning to you too ego I say aloud.

Good morning Mrs. Mitchell says the Valet as he opens the door. Good morning Rafael while tipping him. The phone rings again its Phil, "hello Phil, sorry I missed your call I was in the elevator." "Okay because I got an emergency call from the satellite office in Blythe, Arizona that will require me to be there for two days and I must leave within an hour for briefing" Phil says. Wow! You haven't been in that office since you were promoted six years ago. Tell Barbara I said

"Hello" and I'll see you in ten minutes. Okay hun I'll see you when you get here, says Phil.

Oh my goodness KCSB is jamming early this morning with old school Reggae.

Singing along with the radio, "she's still loving me though I caused her so much pain I've done my share of wrong, time and time again." Whew! That Morgan Heritage is the bomb. I pull into the three car garage and see Phil loading his pride and joy he calls Blackie which is a Dodge Durango.

Honey, I'm home! I yell out to Phil. A voice comes from inside the Truck "I'm in the backseat I'll be right out." Did that brother just hide a pillow and blanket in the back of the truck, girlfriend? Okay ego, you up real early aren't you, I say. He can hide anything he wants right about now he will get hit so hard in a few weeks, he'll think a Tsunami hit his ass.

Can I help you with something Phil? Phil stutters, uh uh nnnooo I got it, thanks. "Bitch, he can't even sneak and do his dirt without showing his nervousness. Oh! His ass will be in for it" says my ego. Okay, I'll see you when you come inside I say as I walk into the kitchen through the garage. I notice a robust aroma as I walk further into our home. Sniff, sniff did you cook dinner that smells delicious, hun? Yes, babe it's all been put away since you worked late. I cooked mom's raspberry glazed chicken wings, Zucchini and wild rice says Phil.

I really have to get going hun, Phil says while grabbing his last bag to load into the truck. Ok, I'm in the restroom come here! Phil walks into the restroom and kisses me on the forehead and says "I'll call you when I arrive in about three hours. "Okay, please be careful don't forget to give Barbara my regards to her and the family." I won't forget says Phil as he walks to his truck.

Suddenly my face don's a big smile… and my wheels are turning in my head then the old faithful ego steps in and says "Go get yo' girl and bring her home for the night." Without warning, I release a loud giggle then tell my ego to go back to sleep… I don't need your help I say.

I jump in the shower and turn in for the night. With pillow tucked between my thighs I smile at the anticipation of seeing Diamond in just a few hours. I tussle and tussle with trying to falling asleep with no success so I just get up and pack my bag for my trip to Fresno to see the new house.

It's four in the morning and I'm still wide awake even after packing bags and checking emails. Hey Ms. Bitch umm do you know why you can't sleep? You didn't feed us that food Phil cooked, says my ego. Acknowledging, I respond he probably laced that shit with some Mop n'glo or some shit trying to kill my ass before he get called to the carpet on his shit with Margo.

I'll have to discard that before I meet Diamond but my ass sure is hungry. I make my way down the spiraling staircase to the kitchen then I hear my cellphone ringing upstairs just as I reach the bottom step. Who could be calling me this time of morning? I ignore the phone for now and continue to the kitchen, surveying the refrigerator to see what I can eat nothing jumps out at me so I grab some Fiber One cereal and put Phil's cooked food in a plastic bag to take curb side with the rest of the trash.

I return upstairs to lie down. In the next three hours I have to get on the road to meet Diamond then off to Fresno. Oh, let me check to see who called, hmph why is Janice calling me this time of morning? There must be something wrong. Wrestling with the idea of calling her back or just trying to get some rest, I decide, oh, what the hell I'll see what's on her mind at this hour, hell, I better call her now because I sure as hell won't be calling anyone when I get back to Diamond. Girlfriend what's going on and why are you calling me at this time of morning?

Well I know Phil not home because I just saw him on the freeway and I wanted to check on you to see if my home girl is aiight, Janice says. Laughing hysterically, Janice what makes you think your girl can't get down with the throw down when I need to… but thanks for having my back. I know you can scrap bitch but you don't want to break those nails of yours because your nail tech is off the chain when it comes to getting you in for repairs. I know but Daijah is the best in the area and she stays open til Midnight.

As Janice precedes with her normal chatter about nothing, my ego chimes in, okay it's time for you to close your fucking eyes or somebody will think you did have a scrap session. Well, Janice again I thank you but I got to get some sleep because I've got a long day ahead of me. Let's do lunch next week. You treating, right Ms. Thang, cause you know you my purse frowns at your Prada taste buds in restaurant choices, Janice replies. Janice if you would stay away from the Vegas strip maybe you can see the money you work so hard for every two weeks. But yes, my treat. Talk to you later… Ahhh!!! Down feathered pillows never felt better under your head than when you're just beyond exhausted. Finally she's asleep now I can get some rest too, the ego exerted.

Fifteen minutes pass and riiiiiinnnnnnggggg!!!!!!! goes the alarm clock which is set to the time that Phil gets up for work. Naturally, it scared the shit out of me so I slam my hand on top of the clock to shut it up but instead I knock it off the nightstand and am forced to jump out of sleep. Clank, clank, vroom vroom as the garbage trucks are picking up cans from the neighbors yards. Ugh, hell no! I am not a happy camper when the keeper of all of this don't get his sleep, its' going to be a rough day and anybody that gets in my way I'll be forced to let them have it. Grunting in frustration, stretching and yawning I peel myself away from the bed dragging myself into the shower to prepare to meet up with Diamond. What the hell, clearly I'm not going to get any rest, so why not get an early start.

Ahhh, steamy hot showers are the best, I say aloud as I lather up my washcloth and begin to sing at the top of my lungs "I've found love on a two-way street and lost it on a lonely highway." That's my jam they don't make music like that anymore, today's music doesn't make sense whatsoever. Okay I'm clean, dressed and ready to go meet my baby. Mmm, I didn't hear from Phil yet and I'm none the wiser. Wonder what he's really up to. He thinks he's got game, only on the basketball court Boo-Boo. Okay get in check ego not today and please behave I know you're sleep deprived but this is a special day for me.

Let me call Diamond to tell her to meet in the lobby in ten minutes. Hello my beautiful Diamond did you get any sleep? She responds "I sure did what about you?" Ha, we won't go there but meet me in the lobby in ten minutes I'm on the expressway now. Ava I'm in the mood for some jazzy poetry do you know of any spots like that in the area Diamond asks. Wow! It's been a while but let's see if **"The Introspect"** is still open when we get situated on our trip. I am approaching your hotel make your way downstairs now.

...7...

Poetry Slam

I arrive at the hotel to see Diamond all smiles standing in the lobby dressed in a hot pink sundress with matching sandals. Diamond makes her way into the car making eye contact the whole way with smile in tow. Hi lovely I say as I reach over to kiss her. Where are we going that we have to leave so early? You're my passenger just sit back and enjoy the ride, I'm in control.

After riding for an hour I'm starting to feel the lack of sleep and without warning, I begin to yawn. Um did you get any rest last night Ava? Well I tried but I was too busy thinking and then Janice called me so I really didn't get too much sleep. Ahh! We're at our destination. Umm, who lives here Diamond asks as we get out of the car and are greeted by a tall, handsome black man that reminded us both of Dwayne "The Rock" Johnson.

Hello ladies my name is Ace Cummings of Ace Realty come in and let me show you around he says walking toward the house. What you see here is a seven bedroom, four and a half bath, six-thousand square feet under air which sits on eight acres of land with room to build. Diamond is gazing in complete awe. Her eyes wide open, head tilted upward to the vaulted ceilings as we walked into the room that was designated as the media-library room equipped with surround sound and theatre seats. I said "Mr. Cummings, I don't need to see anymore I'm sold and so is this house."

Confused, Diamond whips her head around to look at me and says "come again?!"

Mr. Cummings can you please excuse us a moment so we can speak privately? As he walks away, I pull Diamond aside and say to her "when you move to California and are my woman forever, this will be our home."

Diamond passes out in my arms. Umm, Mr. Cummings can you come in and give me a hand putting her on the sofa? Mr. Cummings comes rushing in and says "what happened? Was the news too much to handle?" he chuckles. I guess she just wasn't expecting to hear my proposal. So Mrs. Mitchell is it safe to say we're closing the deal on this beaut today as they struggle lifting dead weight onto the sofa. Yes, it's a done deal and if you can speak to the interior designer who staged this home I will pay them half of what it cost them to furnish the home in cash in two days we'll have the sweetest deal ever. He says you're kidding…. Pausing… He continues "let me get this right you want the entire home AS IS including the furniture and accessories. A faint moaning in the background is heard. Its Diamond coming back to consciousness… am I dreaming she says?

Correct Mr. Cummings, when do you think you can get back to me on that because I'm ready to get things rolling as quickly as possible? I believe I can make a few phone calls now if you have the time he says. Of course I'm available for the next two hours so make those calls and I'll show myself around the rest of the place. Diamond, are you okay to walk around to see the rest of our home? She rises to her feet and follows me to the Master bathroom to see the Roman tub nestled underneath a window overlooking a garden with beautiful flowers of all colors and a gazebo.

Ava are you serious, are you buying this for us to live here together or are you buying this for me to stay in alone and you come when you can get away from Phil? I guess you'll have to wait and see but this is where we'll spend plenty of days and nights until then let's look around. Mrs. Mitchell, make sure you see the door next to the pantry in the kitchen, yells Mr. Cummings.

Ladies! Mr. Cummings yelled as he opens the door to the mystery room next to the pantry. We both gasped in amazement at a fully equipped workout room with top of the line equipment to include high end weights system that you only see in the gyms that we pay monthly membership fees to. I already see you will be spending time in this room especially since the speaker system and flat screen TV's are in place says Diamond.

Mr. Cummings I say excitedly, do you have a SOLD sign in your trunk because this house is ours as of this very moment. Why of course I do he replies. Let's get the paperwork started and I'll give you this check for all of the furnishings. Would Two Million Dollars cover all expenses? Indeed it does. Then it's settled. I call out to Diamond to give her the great news but she's not responding due to shock. I find her standing in the corner of the living room gazing up at the chandelier that's suspended in a vaulted tray ceiling, which is catching the rays of the sun through its dangling crystals.

Diamond asks is this a dream or a practical joke? Oh I know Ashton Kutcher is going to pop out and say "YOU'VE BEEN PUNKED." Laughing uncontrollably, I reply "you actually watched that show"?! I grab her hands, gaze into those beautiful eyes and tell her no my dear this is not a punked prank this is where we will share the rest of our lives together… 1600 West Haven Lane. Now, let's go to this new Spoken word spot called Out Loud not far from here to celebrate. Over the tears Diamond replies "okay that should be nice to do tonight."

Night falls and there's a crisp breeze in the air as we cross the vast walkway of the courtyard that leads to the indoor swimming pool of our new house. Mr. Cummings walks over to us and hands me the paperwork and the keys and says "Congratulations and welcome to your new home." Thank you so much for everything Mr. Cummings. Diamond and I escort him to the front door. Diamond would you bring the car to the front the keys are on the kitchen counter then we can head down to Out Loud. Mrs. Mitchell it's truly been a pleasure to have done business with you and my significant other told me you would love this house says Mr. Cummings. Your significant other has taste tell him I thank him too. I found myself blushing and I close the front door.

Don't you just love the night breeze Diamond? Yes, it is refreshing but what tops it off is the company that the breeze lifts as if through me. Ava, I am so in awe and speechless at what you've done to bring us together. As we pull up in the parking lot of the club we notice a crowd of women rushing towards the door. Curious, I asked "what's the rush" to the closest young lady that can hear my voice and she replied Lady B is performing and she always packs the place. Well in that case young lady you save me a booth by the time I get inside your first three drinks are on me. The young lady yells as she approaches the door "Are you serious Ms.?" I respond "get me a booth and you'll have three drinks of your choice on me." That woman disappeared quick babe says Diamond, I laugh hysterically and reply I guess she's thirsty.

We finally arrive at the entrance of the club and we're greeted instantly as if there was red carpet affair going on inside. Wow! The young lady is waving her arms frantically as to direct us to our booth she saved for us right up front. As we make our way to the booth we grab the attention of the barmaid to pay up my end of the deal of three free drinks. As we take our seats, we thank the young lady then introduce ourselves. I'm Ava and this is Diamond oddly enough, my reputation precedes me and the young lady already knows who I am.

She says her name is Evelyn Waters, surprised, I ask Evelyn Waters as in last years voted the youngest COO of Waters and Waters law firm. Bashfully she responds yes that is me, Diamond says "the youngest COO just how young are you?" I'm Thirty-Six years young."

The club emcee is approaching the stage making her way through the crowd slapping the hands of the patrons. Ladies and gentlemen are you ready for what's in store for you tonight?

The crowd screaming "Yes and clapping hands"

Alrighty then without further ado we welcome to the stage all the way from Buffalo, New York the talented woman that will tell you like it is about yo ass, ladies and gentlemen The one and only Eclectic.

Eclectic: Wuddup up Cali people grab onto your seats tonight because wrecks in effect there are some awesome acts coming up that's got some shit they want to get off their chest, son. This piece was written last year and it's called Bi-Curious. The crowd giggles, oh don't act brand new up in this shit everybody in this room has thought about it, tried it, wanted to try it and for all we know it's about fifteen of ya'll doing the shit on the down low. Eclectic chuckles then proceeds to cite her work.

Bi-Curious

She was bi-curious with bi-sexual tendencies
She had yearnings and cravings that only a
Woman could please…
(Shush)Secretly!
Yearnings that caused her to squeeze…
And tap her feet
Adjust herself in her seat
Ball her fist upon her knees
And struggle for composure
As she clinched her teeth.
Cravings that put her in frenzy…
Crushing and lusting
Tingling and trembling without
Understanding the meaning of that
Which she was feigning she had a hunger
Of wonder
She had been harboring a fascination
For the female part
Concave, for the perception a fitting pot
Safe in the sanctities of her home
She began to moan
As her fingers gently roamed the suppleness
Of each breast
Her nipples coupled between her fingers arrest
She closed her eyes with legs spread wide
She took her hand between her thighs and exploited the
Fullness between her hips
And … all… of… it's… Thickness

Bi-curiously exasperated she masturbated
With these female imageries she self-fornicated
And effectually consummated self-rape
There was nothing pure or innocent
About her thoughts
Or the urges and actions that she half-ass fought
Confused and surprised unwilling to completely
Comprehend the pleasures that lay upon her face
Truth was on the horizon dawning a new day
She was bi-curious with bi-sexual tendencies
She had yearnings and cravings that only a
Woman could please…
(Shush) Secretly!

The crowd applauds and screams at the top of their lungs asking for more. The Emcee returns to the stage giving dap to Eclectic then says to the audience "You not ready for more of that shit" well coming up next to the stage we have a local gentleman who relocated here all the way from Key West, Florida. Ladies and gentleman welcome Jay Risbane to the stage.

While Jay does his thing, the barmaid returns to take our order. Hello ladies what can I get you to drink tonight? I'll have two glasses of Corton-Charlemagne Grand Cru and Evelyn what are you having Ava asks, I'll have a Cosmopolitan. I thank you for the drinks Mrs. Mitchell, please call me Ava and a deal is a deal. The crowd gets loud with excitement after Jay's performance as the Emcee returns to introduce the next performer.

Diamond are you enjoying yourself thus far Ava asks, responding after what you've already done what else is there to do but enjoy myself she replied. Ladies and gentlemen I present to you straight from Compton, California welcome to the stage Lady B and the B stands for none other than Bodacious!

Lady Bodacious: What's going on LA how are you doing this lovely night are you ready as I close out tonight with a couple of pieces.

Mistress

Pull up a chair baby
Let me bend your ear
We been doing this thing
For almost three years and now
You're here telling me
That there's a tragedy
In the midst of me
Cuz you want to leave this life we've lived...
You're not happy I get it
Irreconcilable differences, I get it
It hurts like hell but I damn I get it
But you see the plot thickens...
They say the easiest way to get over an old love is to get under a new
And I see that's what you've chosen to do
So you choose her and leave me
And I'm left here with nothing but a memory
Of what used to be
Painfully wondering...
What happened to the promises you made of forever
But I digress
See my real beef is this
You made her your lover
And you're making me your mistress
What the fuck is this?

(((Reeeeeeewwwwwiiiiiindddddddd

The crowd yells!! Lady B laughs, "Oh y'all feelin' that shit huh. Lady B rewinds the audiences selected part of her writings then continues with her craft)))

There's another on your arm
Vying for your affection
And though the best of me
Chooses not to compete
I can't help what's happening
Inside of me
That part of me
That needs to be
Your Mrs. And not your mistress
You see
I was yours before she came to be
I had your love you had my heart
So I refuse to be downgraded
Set aside waiting with baited breath
For the next moment you choose...
Choose to come around
Like a thief in the night
To steal the jewel between my thighs
Then leave me pleasingly
Only to call her immediately
To whisper sweet nothings in her ear
No I can't dare
I refuse to live there
In misery knowing that you'd likely be
With her momentarily
Your Mistress???
That one who came into a previously established union

And broke apart what you built with her...
Little remorse, little guilt
Because you see for just this moment it isn't she you want it's me.
Should that make me feel empowered?
Because if but for one hour
All you see is me seductively, enticing, exciting
And riding you off into bliss
Man miss me with that shit.
You leave me for her
Yet return to me for pleasure, why?
Does she not measure?
Measure up to all you thought she would be
Cuz while you fucking her
Your pussy's yearning for me
Do you not see?
It's my name that's been tattooed
On that well deep within you
From nights of endless pleasure...
I never, no I never...
Never forgot to ensure your thorough satisfaction...
Your reaction, your reaction, your reaction
Was always damn girl how did you learn to rock my world?
So good like that
Never had it like that
Oh baby, please keep it like that
Make me explode... Like... That...
Damn that!
Baby you gotta choose because you stand to lose
All that this is, has been and could be

Because I refuse
To be misused cuz you're moving forward to her
While reaching back for me
Please...
With this world wracked with disease
HIV's and STD's you think I'm gonna stay on my knees
Pleasing you the way I do willingly ingesting her residue
That's been left inside of you from the night before when you...
When you made her feel like she's your world
Then turn around for another taste of your former girl
What is this?
You and me I think of longingly
You're still so deep inside of me
And that's why this shit has me in agony
Don't want you to leave
But still I can't be... I refuse to be...
Too good to be... Never used to be...
Your mistress!
---Roaring applause---

That's what's up… Let me take it down a few notches for those folk who found that one a little harder to swallow. This next piece was written during a time in my life when I was mesmerized by the swagger of someone I was dating… this bitch had a swagger that made everyone green with envy because they wanted it but couldn't have, I thought I was the shit too cuz she was mine but hell, not even my ass could compete. This is called "The way you move."

The Way You Move

Baby you've got this way about you
That makes everybody wanna be around you
It's in the way you dress and how you wear your hair
That Chill and sexy way, that calm and cocky air
So Cool and confident
Got swagger for days
You're the shit girl, what more can I say
Dare I not fail to mention
Oh baby you've got my attention
Forgive me if I speak out of turn
But damn these girls gotta learn
How to approach somebody as smooth as you
Something about the way you move
Never fake or phony, never perpetrate
Don't need nobody to validate
In a class all your own
You make the rules
Cool under pressure, no matter what you do
Walk into a room and all heads turn
For a woman like you, hell everybody yearns
Dare I not fail to mention
Oh baby you've got my attention
Forgive me if I speak out of turn
But damn these girls gotta learn
How to approach somebody as smooth as you
Something about the way you move
You got me mesmerized
Got me captivated - Watching you glide

Got my body aching
How do you do that voodoo you do so well
Dare I not fail to mention
Oh baby you've got my attention
Forgive me if I speak out of turn
But damn these girls gotta learn
How to approach somebody as smooth as you
Something about the way you move
---Applause---

What does a young lady have to do for a drink around here I'm getting parched like a mother fucker up here under these damn spotlights, hell my name ain't J-Hud. A voice from the back of the room says "What would you like to drink young lady?" Damn, I know yo ass ain't from Cali speaking all proper and shit pass Lady B a Corona with lime sweetheart. Wiping the sweat from her brow she sees a hand reaching out to give her the Corona with Lime. In a deep smooth voice the gentleman says "I hope this is cold enough to quench your thirst." Damn, that's some Billy Dee Williams shit right there, show yourself so I can see what fresh meat we have in our state. Lady B holds the hand of the stranger and is immediately blinded by the latest diamond encrusted Bvlgari Astrale watch which runs anywhere from 2-18 Million dollars or more. Lady B clears her throat and manages to whisper "damn."

The stranger introduces himself, "my name is Max and no I'm not from California I am from Baltimore, Maryland." Lady B is so speechless that she forgot she was on stage and had one more piece to perform. Damn, do you see this dark chocolate sexy Ooooo says Lady B.? I'm sorry peeps let me wrap up this last piece and I'm gonna see about getting me a piece of this dark chocolate candy bar a little later.

With Regret

I'm sitting here quietly
When suddenly tears begin to stream
Down my face unexpectedly
And I realize it's of you I think
How can this be?
No more you and me
For eternity
And it pains me
How I failed to see
How unhappy you had become
Repeatedly you told me exactly what you need
And I failed to be... Enough
Failed to measure up
Failed to step it up
Lost in complacency
Thinking that I indeed
Gave you all you need and more
But if that's the case then why have you turned away
Never thought I'd see the day
When I'd here you say
Good-bye
Two words that have broken me down to my knees in misery
Baffled by how I totally missed all the queues
Got caught up in self-praise thinking I was the shit while I shitted on you
Making you feel less than, beneath, beat up and defeated
I treated you poorly now you're leaving me and I'm a mess.
Somehow I forgot to see you...
Now I'm crying cuz I need you

You're there living cuz you chose to
Move on with your life cuz I failed you
And I'm sorry!
Somehow I felt justified
Because you cheated and you lied
But it takes two to spoil this ride and I'm guilty...
Just as guilty as you
Because you see I failed to
Do what was necessary to keep you
Interested...
I missed it...
I failed to realized the heart is controlled by the mind
And if I wanted to keep it
Then I needed to meet it
Where it was located
Because everything else is dictated to
By what's between the eyes
And not what's between the thighs
So to keep you satisfied
I had to take care of your mind
But I didn't...
I bitched and moaned about who knows what
And now I can care less, I don't give a fuck
Cuz none of that shit really measures up
To what I had with you
If I could do it all again
I wouldn't forget
What it takes to keep you happy and free from stress
I'd listen to you more and talk a lot less
I'd show you I trust you and give you my best...
Because that's what you deserve and nothing less
You never asked for much
Never required a lot from me
My patience and love was all you needed
You were a simple love
You weren't complex

But now my opportunity is lost
It's been replaced
With Regret

Applauses get louder and louder followed by the cheers of encore from the entire room. The Emcee returns to the stage…

Ladies and gentlemen I warned you that it was a wreck in effect night… Listen, on behalf of **Out Loud** and myself we thank you for coming out and we expect you to return next week and perhaps we can get an update on Lady B and Sexual Chocolate over there. (Laughter)

After the show we exchange phone numbers with Evelyn then exit the club cackling about tonight's performances. Just then, I'm frightened by the vibration of my cellphone in my pocket. Peaking at the caller ID I notice it's Phil calling from the office number so that just lets me know he's still where he says he is and the call was sent to voicemail. I open the car door by remote, Diamond and I say good night to Evelyn to which she says we must get together so I can redeem my two drinks you two still owe me.

That's right! Yes, I do owe you two more drinks what about you come over to our place next Saturday and we'll settle our deal over some good food. I would love that Ava what's the address, Evelyn asks. Diamond said I knew that was coming up so I'm writing it down for you as she hands Evelyn the paper with the address on it. Evelyn giggles as she reads the address and says ok neighbors what time is good. Let's say any time after Three O'clock. It was a pleasure ladies good night. Everyone was in their cars awaiting the crowd to move to exit the parking lot so in the meantime Diamond is looking in the mirror refreshing her lipstick and catches a glimpse of Lady B and that Sexy Chocolate leaned up against the building smoking cigarettes.

Where would you like to lay your head at tonight, babe? Diamond asks. Well, considering we have the house on the hill that I share with Phil, the hotel room, and now our newly purchased home in San Fernando just pick one. Let's stay at the new home sweetie, Diamond requested. Ok, we'll have to stop by Kroger's to get some things for breakfast and some toiletries but Haven Lane here we come.

Acknowledgement

Special thanks to Shawn "QueenLyric" of HerART Gallery for your creative contributions to this book, including spoken word pieces Mistress, The Way You Move, and With Regret! Additional thanks for lending your editing skill to helping make this dream a reality!

www.ingramcontent.com/pod-product-compliance
Ingram Content Group UK Ltd.
Pitfield, Milton Keynes, MK11 3LW, UK
UKHW041929190726
13854UKWH00004B/1517

9 781304 748089